TEENY WITCH Goes to SCHOOL

by LIZ MATTHEWS
illustrated by CAROLYN LOH

Troll Associates

This edition published in 2002.

Library of Congress Cataloging-in-Publication Data

Matthews, Liz.
Teeny Witch goes to school / by Liz Matthews; illustrated by
Carolyn Loh.
p. cm.
Summary: Teeny Witch does not want to leave her aunts and spend
the day in school, but after the first day of school she finds it to
be a place of fun.
ISBN 0-8167-2276-5 (lib. bdg.) ISBN 0-8167-2277-3 (pbk.)
[1. Schools—Fiction. 2. Witches—Fiction. 3. Aunts—Fiction.]
I. Loh, Carolyn, ill. II. Title.
PZ7.M4337Ti 1991
[E]—dc20 90-11208

Copyright © 1991 by Troll Associates, Mahwah, N.J.
All rights reserved. No portion of this book may be reproduced in any
form, electronic or mechanical, including photocopying, recording, or
information storage and retrieval systems, without prior written
permission from the publisher. Printed in the U.S.A.
10 9 8 7 6 5

It was a bright sunny morning. It was an important morning for Teeny Witch. Teeny's three witch aunts tiptoed into her room.

"Wake up, Teeny Witch," said Aunt Icky.

"It's seven o'clock," said Aunt Ticky.

"Time to get ready for the first day of school," said Aunt Vicky.

Slowly Teeny Witch opened her eyes.
"Good morning," she said.

"You must be very excited about going to school," said Aunt Ticky.

Teeny did not answer.

"Hurry and get dressed," said Aunt Icky. "You don't want to be late for the first day of school, do you?"

Teeny Witch sat up in bed. "I guess not," she said in a small voice.

“See you at breakfast,” said Aunt Vicky.

Teeny Witch got out of bed. She washed her face. She brushed her teeth and combed her hair. She slowly dressed in the brand-new outfit her aunts had bought for her.

Teeny looked at herself in the mirror. “I look nice,” she said. “But do I really want to go to school?”

Teeny had visited her new school over the summer. The school was nice. Her teacher was nice, too. Teeny was excited about school. But something was bothering her.

"Breakfast is ready, Teeny," called Aunt Vicky.
"Coming," Teeny replied. Teeny trudged out of her room and down to the kitchen.

Usually Teeny loved pancakes. But today she didn't feel like eating. Her stomach felt jiggly.

Aunt Ticky packed Teeny's lunch box.

Aunt Vicky put pencils in Teeny's backpack. They were very excited that Teeny was going to school.

"It's time to go," Aunt Icky told Teeny. Teeny tried to smile, but she couldn't. A big tear rolled down her cheek.

“Teeny, what is wrong?” asked Aunt Ticky.
“It’s school,” Teeny said. “I don’t want to go.
I want to stay home.”

Teeny's aunts were surprised and puzzled. "Why do you want to stay home?" Aunt Vicky asked.

Teeny wiped away her tears. "I won't see you all day," she said. "I will miss you very, very much."

The three witches smiled at Teeny and gave her a big hug.
"We will miss you, too, Teeny," Aunt Icky said. "But you have to go to school. You will have fun. The day will go fast. You will see."

Teeny picked up her lunch box. "If I have to, I will go," Teeny said.

The three aunts drove Teeny to her school bus stop. They all waited for the bus to come.

"Will the day really go fast?" Teeny asked.

Aunt Icky nodded. "School will go fast because it is fun," she said.

"It is so much fun you will hardly even miss us," said Aunt Ticky.

"You won't even think about us while you're at school," Aunt Vicky said.

Just then the school bus pulled up.
Red lights flashed. Teeny kissed
her aunts good-bye.

Teeny waved good-bye.
“I hope Teeny thinks about us just a little,”
Aunt Vicky whispered.

The bus was full of children. Everyone was laughing and giggling. Teeny did not mind the noise. She laughed and giggled, too.

Sitting next to Teeny was a little girl in a pink dress. The little girl smiled at Teeny. “My name is Jenny,” she said.

“My name is Teeny,” said Teeny Witch.

“Let’s be friends,” said Jenny.

“Okay,” said Teeny.

Making a new friend made Teeny feel really good. Jenny and Teeny talked all the way to school. The ride went very fast.

Teeny's teacher, Mrs. Green, was waiting for them.

“Welcome,” she said.
The classroom was bright and cheerful.
“Wow! What a great place,” Teeny said to Jenny.

Mrs. Green let everyone pick a desk. Jenny sat near Teeny.

Teeny liked having her own desk. She put her pencils and papers in her desk. She was so busy she did not think about her aunts.

"Isn't school fun?" Jenny said to Teeny.

Teeny nodded. "I wonder what we will do now?"

"Now we will learn about rules," said Mrs. Green. She told the class about safety rules and good neighbor rules. Teeny listened very carefully. The rules did not seem too hard.

Next the children practiced printing. Teeny wrote her name neatly.

"Very good, Teeny," said Mrs. Green. That made Teeny feel proud.

Soon it was time for lunch. The class walked to the lunchroom. Teeny and Jenny sat at the same table.

"School sure goes fast," said Teeny. "My aunts were right."

After lunch, everyone went out to the playground. Teeny played tag with other boys and girls. Teeny ran very fast. No one could catch Teeny Witch.

Soon it was time to go back inside. Everyone lined up by the door.

"I had lots of fun," Teeny said to Jenny.

"So did I," Jenny replied.

Teeny Witch had fun all day long.
She learned lots of new things.

The best part of the day was art class. Teeny painted a picture. It was a very special picture.

"Your picture is very nice," said Mrs. Green.
"I can't wait until my aunts see it," said Teeny.

After art, it was time to go home. Teeny put her picture in her bag. The bell rang. The children went to their buses.

"Good-bye, children," called Mrs. Green. "See you tomorrow."

Teeny waved. Vroom! The bus drove away.

Teeny's aunts were waiting for her at the bus stop.
"Hi, Aunts!" shouted Teeny as she bounced off the bus.

All the way home, Teeny talked about school. She told her aunts all the things she had done. Teeny's aunts were happy for her.

When they got home, Teeny went to her room.
"Teeny sure had a busy day," said Aunt Icky.
"It sounded like lots of fun," said Aunt Ticky.
"It was so busy and so much fun, Teeny didn't think about us at all," said Aunt Vicky.

The three aunts felt a little sad. They wanted Teeny to have fun. They were glad she liked school so much. But they didn't want Teeny Witch to forget all about them.

Teeny Witch came back into the room. "I have something to show you," Teeny said to her aunts. "I painted a picture in art class. It is a special picture. I painted it for you."

Teeny held up her special picture. It was a picture of her three witch aunts.

The picture made the three aunts feel very happy. Teeny had thought about them at school after all!

"We are very proud of you, Teeny," said Aunt Icky.

"The picture really is special," said Aunt Ticky.

"You are special, too, Teeny Witch," said Aunt Vicky.

Teeny's aunts hung the picture on the wall.
Teeny Witch looked at her picture and smiled. "I can't wait for tomorrow," said Teeny. "Tomorrow I go to school again!"

BYE!
SCHOOL BUS